JAMES

PERCY

MEET ALL THESE FRIENDS IN BUZZ BOOKS:

Thomas the Tank Engine
The Animals of Farthing Wood
Biker Mice From Mars
Winnie-the-Pooh
Fireman Sam
Rupert
Babar

First published in Great Britain 1992 by Buzz Books
an imprint of Reed Children's Books
Michelin House, 81 Fulham Road, London SW3 6RB
and Auckland, Melbourne, Singapore and Toronto
Reprinted 1993 (twice) and 1994 (twice)

Photographs by David Mitton and Terry Permane
for Britt Allcroft's production of
Thomas the Tank Engine and Friends

ISBN 1 85591 222 8

Printed and bound in Italy

PERCY'S PROMISE

buzz books

Every summer the Island of Sodor is very busy. Holidaymakers love to sightsee and when the weather is fine, there is no better place to visit.

Some people like to go to the mountains, others like the valleys.

Children love the seaside.

One morning Thomas was puffing along the line that runs by the coast. His two coaches, Annie and Clarabel, were packed with children going to the beach.

Everyone was happy.

Percy was taking some trucks to the harbour.

"Hello Thomas, you look cheerful. I wish I could take children today instead of trucks."

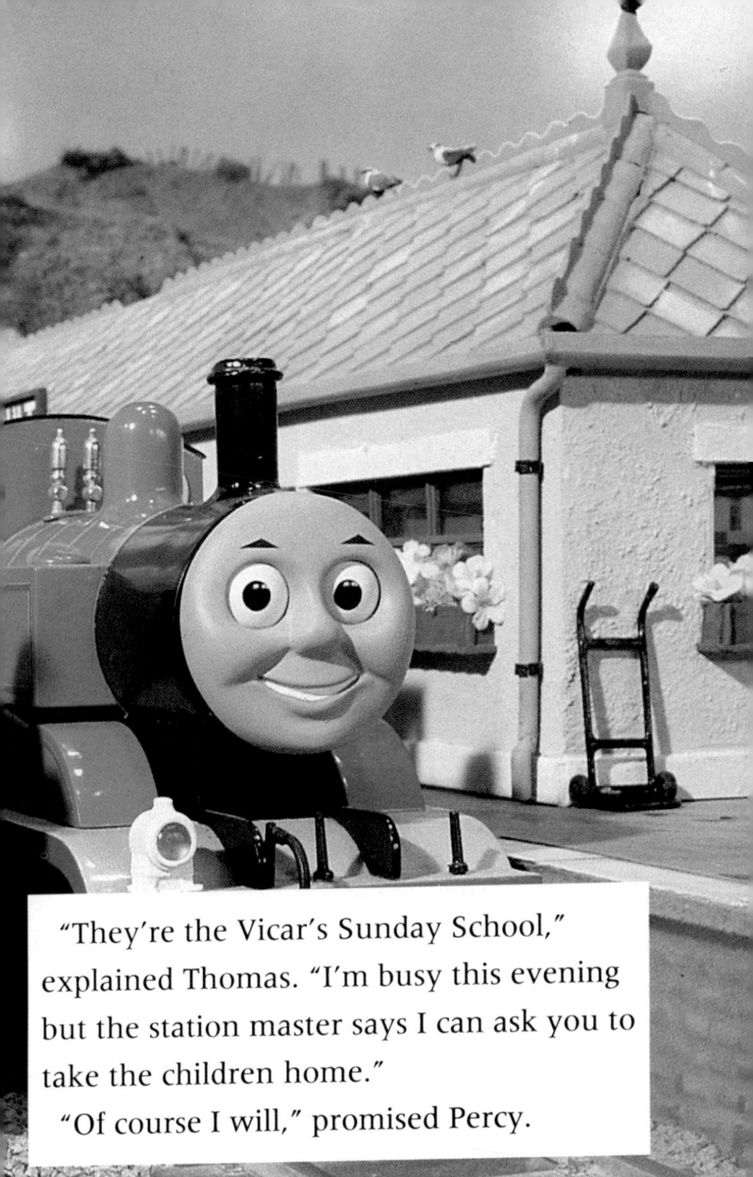

"They're the Vicar's Sunday School," explained Thomas. "I'm busy this evening but the station master says I can ask you to take the children home."

"Of course I will," promised Percy.

Later Percy saw Harold. "Sorry Percy, can't talk. I'm on High Alert."

"Why?"

"Bad weather's due. My help's always needed. Mind how you go, Percy."

"Paah!" huffed Percy. "As long as I've got rails to run on, I can go anywhere - in any weather - anyhow. Goodbye."

He set off for the beach.

It was a beautiful day but Edward was worried.

"Be careful," he warned. "There's a storm coming."

"A promise is a promise," thought Percy, "no matter what the weather."

The children had a lovely day but by teatime dark clouds loomed ahead.

Annie and Clarabel were glad when Percy arrived. He was just in time.

The rain streamed down Percy's boiler.

"Ugh." He shivered and thought of his nice dry shed.

Percy struggled on past coastal villages and into the countryside. The river was rising fast.

"I wish I could see, I wish I could see," complained Percy as he battled against the rain.

More trouble lay ahead.

"Oh," hissed Percy, "the water is sloshing my fire."

Percy's driver and fireman had to find some more firewood.

"I'll have some of your floorboards please," said the fireman to the guard.

"I only swept the floor this morning," grumbled the guard, but he still helped.

Soon Percy's fire was burning well. He felt warm and comfortable again.

Then he saw Harold.

"Oh dear," thought Percy. "Harold's come to laugh at me."

Something thudded onto Percy's boiler.

"Ow!" exclaimed Percy. "He needn't throw things."

"It's a parachute," laughed his driver. "Harold's dropping hot drinks for us."

"Thank you Harold," whistled Percy.

"Good to be of service," replied Harold and buzzed away.

6

The water lapped Percy's wheels. Percy was losing steam again but he plunged bravely on.

"I promised," he panted. "I promised."

He made one more big effort and, at last, exhausted but triumphant, he brought the train home.

"Well done Percy," cheered Thomas. "You kept your promise despite everything."

The Fat Controller arrived in Harold. First he thanked the men, then Percy.

"Harold told me you were -er - wizard. He says he can beat you at some things, but not at being a submarine. I don't know what you two get up to sometimes, but I do know that you're a Really Useful Engine."

"Oh Sir," whispered Percy happily.

THOMAS
1

EDWARD
2

GORDON